A Note to Parents and Caregivers:

Read-it! Readers are for children who are just starting on the amazing road to reading. These beautiful books support both the acquisition of reading skills and the love of books.

 The PURPLE LEVEL presents basic topics and objects using high frequency words and simple language patterns.

 The RED LEVEL presents familiar topics using common words and repeating sentence patterns.

 The BLUE LEVEL presents new ideas using a larger vocabulary and varied sentence structure.

 The YELLOW LEVEL presents more challenging ideas, a broad vocabulary, and wide variety in sentence structure.

 The GREEN LEVEL presents more complex ideas, an extended vocabulary range, and expanded language structures.

 The ORANGE LEVEL presents a wide range of ideas and concepts using challenging vocabulary and complex language structures.

When sharing a book with your child, read in short stretches, pausing often to talk about the pictures. Have your child turn the pages and point to the pictures and familiar words. And be sure to reread favorite stories or parts of stories.

There is no right or wrong way to share books with children. Find time to read with your child, and pass on the legacy of literacy.

Adria F. Klein, Ph.D.
Professor Emeritus
California State University
San Bernardino, California

Managing Editor: Bob Temple
Creative Director: Terri Foley
Editor: Peggy Henrikson
Editorial Adviser: Andrea Cascardi
Copy Editor: Laurie Kahn
Designer: Nathan Gassman
Page production: Picture Window Books
The illustrations in this book were rendered with watercolor.

Picture Window Books
5115 Excelsior Boulevard
Suite 232
Minneapolis, MN 55416
1-877-845-8392
www.picturewindowbooks.com

Printed in the United States of America.

Library of Congress Cataloging-in-Publication Data
Blackaby, Susan.
The princess and the pea / by Hans Christian Andersen ; adapted by Susan
Blackaby ; illustrated by Charlene DeLage.
p. cm. — (Read-it! readers fairy tales)
Summary: By feeling a pea through twenty mattresses and twenty
feather beds, a girl proves that she is a real princess.
ISBN 1-4048-0223-1
[1. Fairy tales.] I. DeLage, Charlene, 1944– ill. II. Andersen, H. C.
(Hans Christian), 1805–1875. Prindsessen paa aerten. English.
III. Title. IV. Series.
PZ8.B5595 Pr 2004
[E]—dc21
                                                        2003006115

The Princess and the Pea

by Hans Christian Andersen

Adapted by Susan Blackaby
Illustrated by Charlene DeLage

Reading Advisors:
Adria F. Klein, Ph.D.
Professor Emeritus, California State University
San Bernardino, California

Kathy Baxter, M.A.
Former Coordinator of Children's Services
Anoka County (Minnesota) Library

Susan Kesselring, M.A.
Literacy Educator
Rosemount-Apple Valley-Eagan (Minnesota) School District

PICTURE WINDOW BOOKS
Minneapolis, Minnesota

Once upon a time, a noble king and a wise queen had a son. He was a fine young prince.

When it came time for the prince to marry, he had to find a wife.

"I can't marry just any old princess,"
said the prince. "I have to find
a *real* princess."

The prince traveled from place to place. He met many, many princesses.

All of them were very nice.

But the prince could not tell which

of them were real princesses.

None of them seemed quite right.

The prince looked and looked and looked and *looked*. He looked all over the world, with no luck at all.

The prince was very sad.

"I'd like to marry a real princess,"

he said. "But I can't find one!"

11

One winter night
a huge storm blew in.

Thunder boomed. Lightning flashed.
It rained like crazy!

Suddenly, there came a knock
at the castle gate. It barely
could be heard above the storm.
"Who's there?" asked the king.

14

"A princess," said a sweet voice.

"A princess!" the king exclaimed.

He opened the gate at once.

There stood a wet, muddy girl.

Her hair streamed like seaweed.

Her clothes were soaked.

Water flowed out of her shoes.

"Oh, my! Look at this poor princess!" said the king.

"Are you a real princess?" asked the prince.

"Of course I am," said the princess.
"I'm just a bit messy."

"I'm not so sure she's real,"
thought the queen. "But I
know just how to find out."

The queen sneaked off
to the bedroom. She removed
all the bedding. Then she put
a green pea on the bed.

The queen put 20 mattresses
on top of the pea. Then she
put 20 feather beds on top
of the mattresses.

The queen returned to the princess.

"Your bedroom is all set," she said.

"Thank you," said the tired princess.

The princess climbed up into bed.
"Sleep tight!" said the queen.

In the morning, the princess came down to breakfast. She greeted the king and queen.

"How did you sleep?" asked the queen.

"Bad, bad, bad!" said the princess.

"I didn't close my eyes. I tossed and turned all night! There was a bump in my bed."

"It was as hard as a rock!
It was as big as an elephant!
I'm black-and-blue all over!
I feel horrible!"

"How delightful!" said the queen.
"Only a real princess would feel
a little pea through all that fluff."

The prince was thrilled.
"I have found my real
princess at last!" he said.

The prince and the princess
were married the next day.

The pea was placed on display
in the royal hall.

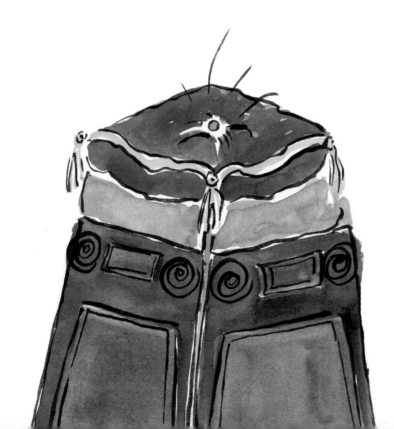

More *Read-it!* Readers

Bright pictures and fun stories help you practice your reading skills. Look for more books at your level.

Beauty and the Beast 1-4048-0981-3

Brave Little Tailor, The 1-4048-0315-7

Bremen Town Musicians, The 1-4048-0310-6

Emperor's New Clothes 1-4048-0224-X

Frog Prince, The 1-4048-0313-0

Hansel and Gretel 1-4048-0316-5

Little Mermaid, The 1-4048-0221-5

Puss in Boots 1-4048-0591-5

Rapunzel 1-4048-0982-1

Rumpelstiltskin 1-4048-0311-4

Shoemaker and His Elves, The 1-4048-0314-9

Steadfast Soldier, The 1-4048-0226-6

Thumbelina 1-4048-0225-8

Tom Thumb 1-4048-0593-1

Ugly Duckling, The 1-4048-0222-3

Wolf and the Seven Little Kids, The 1-4048-0594-X

Looking for a specific title or level? A complete list of *Read-it!* Readers is available on our Web site:
www.picturewindowbooks.com